The Cost of Kindness

By

Jerome K. Jerome

British Library Cataloguing-in-Publication Data
A catalogue record for this book is available from the
British Library

Jerome K. Jerome

Jerome Klapka Jerome was born in Walsall, England in 1859. Both his parents died while he was in his early teens, and he was forced to quit school to support himself. Jerome worked for a number of years collecting coal along railway tracks, before trying his hand at acting, journalism, teaching and soliciting. At long last, in 1885, he had some success with *On the Stage – and Off,* a comic memoir of his experiences with an acting troupe. Jerome produced a number of essays over the following years, and married in 1888, spending the honeymoon in "a little boat" on the Thames.

In 1889, Jerome published his most successful and best-remembered work, *Three Men in a Boat.* Featuring himself and two of his friends encountering humorous situations while floating down the Thames in a small boat, the book was an instant success, and has never been out of print. In fact, its popularity was such that the number of registered Thames boats went up fifty percent in the year following its publication. With the financial security provided by *Three Men in a Boat,* Jerome was able to dedicate himself fully to writing, producing eleven more novels and a number of anthologies of short fiction.

In 1926, Jerome published his autobiography, *My Life and Times.* He died a year later, aged 68.

"Kindness," argued little Mrs. Pennycoop, "costs nothing."

"And, speaking generally, my dear, is valued precisely at cost price," retorted Mr. Pennycoop, who, as an auctioneer of twenty years' experience, had enjoyed much opportunity of testing the attitude of the public towards sentiment.

"I don't care what you say, George," persisted his wife; "he may be a disagreeable, cantankerous old brute—I don't say he isn't. All the same, the man is going away, and we may never see him again."

"If I thought there was any fear of our doing so," observed Mr. Pennycoop, "I'd turn my back on the Church of England to-morrow and become a Methodist."

"Don't talk like that, George," his wife admonished him, reprovingly; "the Lord might be listening to you."

"If the Lord had to listen to old Cracklethorpe He'd sympathize with me," was the opinion of Mr. Pennycoop.

"The Lord sends us our trials, and they are meant for our good," explained his wife. "They are meant to teach us patience."

"You are not churchwarden," retorted her husband; "you can get away from him. You hear him when he is in the pulpit, where, to a certain extent, he is bound to keep his temper."

"You forget the rummage sale, George," Mrs. Pennycoop reminded him; "to say nothing of the church decorations."

"The rummage sale," Mr. Pennycoop pointed out to her, "occurs only once a year, and at that time your own temper, I have noticed—"

"I always try to remember I am a Christian," interrupted little Mrs. Pennycoop. "I do not pretend to be a saint, but whatever I say I am always sorry for it afterwards—you know I am, George."

"It's what I am saying," explained her husband. "A vicar who has contrived in three years to make every member of his congregation hate the very sight of a church—well, there's something wrong about it somewhere."

Mrs. Pennycoop, gentlest of little women, laid her plump and still pretty hands upon her husband's shoulders. "Don't think, dear, I haven't sympathized with you. You have borne it nobly. I have marvelled sometimes that you have been able to control yourself as you have done, most times; the things that he has said to you."

Mr. Pennycoop had slid unconsciously into an attitude suggestive of petrified virtue, lately discovered.

"One's own poor self," observed Mr. Pennycoop, in accents of proud humility—"insults that are merely personal one can put up with. Though even there," added the senior churchwarden, with momentary descent towards the plane of human nature, "nobody cares to have it hinted publicly across the vestry table that one has chosen to collect from the left side for the express purpose of artfully passing over one's own family."

"The children have always had their three-penny-bits ready waiting in their hands," explained Mrs. Pennycoop, indignantly.

"It's the sort of thing he says merely for the sake of making a disturbance," continued the senior churchwarden. "It's the things he does I draw the line at."

"The things he has done, you mean, dear," laughed the little woman, with the accent on the "has." "It is all over now, and we are going to be rid of him. I expect, dear, if we only knew, we should find it was his liver. You know, George, I remarked to you the first day that he came how pasty he looked and what a singularly unpleasant mouth he had. People can't help these things, you know, dear. One should look upon them in the light of afflictions and be sorry for them."

"I could forgive him doing what he does if he didn't seem to enjoy it," said the senior churchwarden. "But, as you say, dear, he is going, and all I hope and pray is that we never see his like again."

"And you'll come with me to call upon him, George," urged kind little Mrs. Pennycoop. "After all, he has been our vicar for three years, and he must be feeling it, poor man—whatever he may pretend—going away like this, knowing that everybody is glad to see the back of him."

"Well, I sha'n't say anything I don't really feel," stipulated Mr. Pennycoop.

"That will be all right, dear," laughed his wife, "so long as you don't say what you do feel. And we'll both of us keep our temper," further suggested the little woman, "whatever happens. Remember, it will be for the last time."

Little Mrs. Pennycoop's intention was kind and Christianlike. The Rev. Augustus Cracklethorpe would be quitting Wychwood-on-the-Heath the following Monday, never to set foot—so the Rev. Augustus Cracklethorpe himself and every single member of his congregation hoped sincerely—in the neighbourhood again. Hitherto no pains had been taken on either side to disguise the mutual joy with which the parting was looked forward to. The Rev. Augustus Cracklethorpe, M.A., might possibly have been of service to his Church in, say, some East-end parish of unsavoury reputation, some mission station far advanced amid the hordes of heathendom. There his inborn instinct of antagonism to everybody and everything surrounding him, his unconquerable disregard for other people's views and feelings, his inspired conviction that everybody but himself was bound to be always wrong about everything, combined with determination to act and speak fearlessly in such belief, might have found their uses. In picturesque little Wychwood-on-the-Heath, among the Kentish hills, retreat beloved of the retired tradesman, the spinster of moderate means, the reformed Bohemian developing latent instincts towards respectability, these qualities made only for scandal and disunion.

For the past two years the Rev. Cracklethorpe's parishioners, assisted by such other of the inhabitants of Wychwood-on-the-Heath as had happened to come into personal contact with the reverend gentleman, had sought to impress upon him, by hints and innuendoes difficult to misunderstand, their cordial and daily-increasing dislike of him, both as a parson and a man. Matters had come to a head by the determination officially announced to him that, failing other alternatives, a deputation of his leading parishioners would wait upon his bishop. This it was that had brought it home to the Rev. Augustus Cracklethorpe that, as the spiritual guide and comforter of Wychwood-on-the Heath, he had proved a failure. The Rev. Augustus had sought and secured the care of other souls. The following Sunday morning he had arranged to preach his farewell sermon, and the occasion promised to be a success from every point of view. Churchgoers who had not visited St. Jude's for months had promised themselves the luxury of feeling they were listening to the Rev. Augustus Cracklethorpe for the last time. The Rev. Augustus Cracklethorpe had prepared a sermon that for plain speaking and directness was likely to leave an impression. The parishioners of St. Jude's, Wychwood-on-the-Heath, had their failings, as we all have. The Rev. Augustus flattered himself that he had not missed out a single one, and was looking forward with pleasurable anticipation to the sensation that his remarks, from his "firstly" to his "sixthly and lastly," were likely to create.

What marred the entire business was the impulsiveness of little Mrs. Pennycoop. The Rev. Augustus Cracklethorpe, informed in his study on the Wednesday afternoon that Mr. and Mrs. Pennycoop had called, entered the drawing-room a quarter of an hour later, cold and severe; and, without offering to shake hands, requested to be informed as shortly as possible for what purpose he had been disturbed. Mrs. Pennycoop had had her speech ready to her tongue. It was just what it should have been, and no more.

It referred casually, without insisting on the point, to the duty incumbent upon all of us to remember on occasion we were Christians; that our privilege it was to forgive and forget; that, generally speaking, there are faults on both sides; that partings should never take place in anger; in short, that little Mrs. Pennycoop and

George, her husband, as he was waiting to say for himself, were sorry for everything and anything they may have said or done in the past to hurt the feelings of the Rev. Augustus Cracklethorpe, and would like to shake hands with him and wish him every happiness for the future. The chilling attitude of the Rev. Augustus scattered that carefully-rehearsed speech to the winds. It left Mrs. Pennycoop nothing but to retire in choking silence, or to fling herself upon the inspiration of the moment and make up something new. She choose the latter alternative.

At first the words came halting. Her husband, man-like, had deserted her in her hour of utmost need and was fumbling with the door-knob. The steely stare with which the Rev. Cracklethorpe regarded her, instead of chilling her, acted upon her as a spur. It put her on her mettle. He should listen to her. She would make him understand her kindly feeling towards him if she had to take him by the shoulders and shake it into him. At the end of five minutes the Rev. Augustus Cracklethorpe, without knowing it, was looking pleased. At the end of another five Mrs. Pennycoop stopped, not for want of words, but for want of breath. The Rev. Augustus Cracklethorpe replied in a voice that, to his own surprise, was trembling with emotion. Mrs. Pennycoop had made his task harder for him. He had thought to leave Wychwood-on-the-Heath without a regret. The knowledge he now possessed, that at all events one member of his congregation understood him, as Mrs. Pennycoop had proved to him she understood him, sympathized with him—the knowledge that at least one heart, and that heart Mrs. Pennycoop's, had warmed to him, would transform what he had looked forward to as a blessed relief into a lasting grief.

Mr. Pennycoop, carried away by his wife's eloquence, added a few halting words of his own. It appeared from Mr. Pennycoop's remarks that he had always regarded the Rev. Augustus Cracklethorpe as the vicar of his dreams, but misunderstandings in some unaccountable way will arise. The Rev. Augustus Cracklethorpe, it appeared, had always secretly respected Mr. Pennycoop. If at any time his spoken words might have conveyed the contrary impression, that must have arisen from the poverty of our language, which does not lend itself to subtle meanings.

Then following the suggestion of tea, Miss Cracklethorpe, sister to the Rev. Augustus—a lady whose likeness to her brother in all respects was startling, the only difference between them being that while he was clean-shaven she wore a slight moustache—was called down to grace the board. The visit was ended by Mrs. Pennycoop's remembrance that it was Wilhelmina's night for a hot bath.

"I said more than I intended to," admitted Mrs. Pennycoop to George, her husband, on the way home; "but he irritated me."

Rumour of the Pennycoops' visit flew through the parish. Other ladies felt it their duty to show to Mrs. Pennycoop that she was not the only Christian in Wychwood-on-the-Heath. Mrs. Pennycoop, it was feared, might be getting a swelled head over this matter. The Rev. Augustus, with pardonable pride, repeated some of the things that Mrs. Pennycoop had said to him. Mrs. Pennycoop was not to imagine herself the only person in Wychwood-on-the-Heath capable of generosity that cost nothing. Other ladies could say graceful nothings—could say them even better. Husbands dressed in their best clothes and carefully rehearsed were brought in to grace the almost endless procession of disconsolate parishioners hammering at the door of St. Jude's parsonage. Between Thursday morning and Saturday night the Rev. Augustus, much to his own astonishment, had been forced to the conclusion that five-sixths of his parishioners had loved him from the first without hitherto having had opportunity of expressing their real feelings.

The eventful Sunday arrived. The Rev. Augustus Cracklethorpe had been kept so busy listening to regrets at his departure, assurances of an esteem hitherto disguised from him, explanations of seeming discourtesies that had been intended as tokens of affectionate regard, that no time had been left to him to think of other matters. Not till he entered the vestry at five minutes to eleven did recollection of his farewell sermon come to him. It haunted him throughout the service. To deliver it after the revelations of the last three days would be impossible. It was the sermon that Moses might have preached to Pharaoh the Sunday prior to the exodus. To crush with it this congregation of broken-hearted adorers sorrowing for his departure would be inhuman. The Rev. Augustus tried to think of passages that might be selected, altered. There were none. From beginning to end it contained not a single sentence capable of being made to sound pleasant by any ingenuity whatsoever.

The Rev. Augustus Cracklethorpe climbed slowly up the pulpit steps without an idea in his head of what he was going to say. The sunlight fell upon the upturned faces of a crowd that filled every corner of the church. So happy, so buoyant a congregation the eyes of the Rev. Augustus Cracklethorpe had never till that day looked down upon. The feeling came to him that he did not want to leave them. That they did not wish him to go, could he doubt? Only by regarding them as a collection of the most shameless hypocrites ever gathered together under one roof. The Rev. Augustus Cracklethorpe dismissed the passing suspicion as a suggestion of the Evil One, folded the neatly-written manuscript that lay before him on the desk, and put it aside. He had no need of a farewell sermon. The arrangements made could easily be altered. The Rev. Augustus Cracklethorpe spoke from his pulpit for the first time an impromptu.

The Rev. Augustus Cracklethorpe wished to acknowledge himself in the wrong. Foolishly founding his judgment upon the evidence of a few men, whose names there would be no need to mention, members of the congregation who, he hoped, would one day be sorry for the misunderstandings they had caused, brethren whom it was his duty to forgive, he had assumed the parishioners of St. Jude's, Wychwood-on-the-Heath, to have taken a personal dislike to him. He wished to publicly apologize for the injustice he had unwittingly done to their heads and to their hearts. He now had it from their own lips that a libel had been put upon them. So far from their wishing his departure, it was self-evident that his going would inflict upon them a great sorrow. With the knowledge he now possessed of the respect—one might almost say the veneration—with which the majority of that congregation regarded him—knowledge, he admitted, acquired somewhat late—it was clear to him he could still be of help to them in their spiritual need. To leave a flock so devoted would stamp him as an unworthy shepherd. The ceaseless stream of regrets at his departure that had been poured into his ear during the last four days he had decided at the last moment to pay heed to. He would remain with them—on one condition.

There quivered across the sea of humanity below him a movement that might have suggested to a more observant watcher the convulsive clutchings of some drowning man at some chance straw. But the Rev. Augustus Cracklethorpe was thinking of himself.

The parish was large and he was no longer a young man. Let them provide him with a conscientious and energetic curate. He had such a one in his mind's eye, a near relation of his own, who, for a small stipend that was hardly worth mentioning, would, he knew it for a fact, accept the post. The pulpit was not the place in which to discuss these matters, but in the vestry afterwards he would be pleased to meet such members of the congregation as might choose to stay.

The question agitating the majority of the congregation during the singing of the hymn was the time it would take them to get outside the church. There still remained a faint hope that the Rev. Augustus Cracklethorpe, not obtaining his curate, might consider it due to his own dignity to shake from his feet the dust of a parish generous in sentiment, but obstinately close-fisted when it came to putting its hands into its pockets.

But for the parishioners of St. Jude's that Sunday was a day of misfortune. Before there could be any thought of moving, the Rev. Augustus raised his surpliced arm and begged leave to acquaint them with the contents of a short note that had just been handed up to him. It would send them all home, he felt sure, with joy and thankfulness in their hearts. An example of Christian benevolence was among them that did honour to the Church.

Here a retired wholesale clothier from the East-end of London—a short, tubby gentleman who had recently taken the Manor House—was observed to turn scarlet.

A gentleman hitherto unknown to them had signalled his advent among them by an act of munificence that should prove a shining example to all rich men. Mr. Horatio Copper—the reverend gentleman found some difficulty, apparently, in deciphering the name.

"Cooper-Smith, sir, with an hyphen," came in a thin whisper, the voice of the still scarlet-faced clothier.

Mr. Horatio Cooper-Smith, taking—the Rev. Augustus felt confident—a not unworthy means of grappling to himself thus early the hearts of his fellow-townsmen, had expressed his desire to pay for the expense of a curate entirely out of his own pocket. Under these circumstances, there would be no further talk of a farewell between the Rev. Augustus Cracklethorpe and his parishioners. It would be the hope of the Rev. Augustus Cracklethorpe to live and die the pastor of St. Jude's.

A more solemn-looking, sober congregation than the congregation that emerged that Sunday morning from St. Jude's in Wychwood-on-the-Heath had never, perhaps, passed out of a church door.

"He'll have more time upon his hands," said Mr. Biles, retired wholesale ironmonger and junior churchwarden, to Mrs. Biles, turning the corner of Acacia Avenue—"he'll have more time to make himself a curse and a stumbling-block."

"And if this 'near relation' of his is anything like him—"

"Which you may depend upon it is the Case, or he'd never have thought of him," was the opinion of Mr. Biles.

"I shall give that Mrs. Pennycoop," said Mrs. Biles, "a piece of my mind when I meet her."

But of what use was that?